My Love Will
Be With You

My Love Will Be With You

BY LAURA KRAUSS MELMED
ILLUSTRATED BY HENRI SORENSEN

HARPERCOLLINSPUBLISHERS

Library of Congress Cataloging-in-Publication Data

Melmed, Laura Krauss.

My love will be with you / by Laura Krauss Melmed ; illustrated by Henri Sorensen. — 1st ed.

p.   cm.

Summary: A variety of fathers tell their children how much they love them.

ISBN 978-0-06-155260-1 (trade bdg.)   ISBN 978-0-06-155261-8 (lib. bdg.)

[1. Stories in rhyme. 2. Father and child—Fiction. 3. Animals—Fiction.] I. Sorensen, Henri, ill. II. Title.

PZ8.3.M55155My 2009   [E]—dc22   2008019202   CIP   AC

Typography by Rachel Zegar

1 2 3 4 5 6 7 8 9 10

First Edition

To my husband, Allan, father par
excellence of Stephanie, Jonathan, and
Michael; and with warmest memories of
my own father, Morris Krauss.
—L.K.M.

To Safia and Lucia.
—H.S.

Said the father eagle to his child,
"Someday you'll soar through a high mountain pass."

Said the father lion to his child,

"Someday you'll hunt in the long, waving grass."

Said the father otter to his child,

"Someday you'll fish in a crystal clear stream."

Said the father panda to his child,

"Someday you'll snuggle your own cub and dream."

Said the father pigeon to his child,

"Someday you'll swagger and strut in the park."

Said the father badger to his child,

"Someday you'll find your way home in the dark."

Said the father monkey to his child,

"Someday you'll climb to the tops of the trees."

Said the father dolphin to his child,

"Someday you'll swim off to faraway seas."

From now until always I want you to know
My love will be with you wherever you go.